Love is a Blue Tick Hound

and other remedies for the common ache

Audrey Cefaly

A SAMUEL FRENCH ACTING EDITION

SAMUEL FRENCH

FOUNDED 1830

SAMUELFRENCH.COM
SAMUELFRENCH-LONDON.CO.UK

FOR PRODUCTION ENQUIRIES

UNITED STATES AND CANADA
Info@SamuelFrench.com
1-866-598-8449

UNITED KINGDOM AND EUROPE
Plays@SamuelFrench-London.co.uk
020-7255-4302

Each title is subject to availability from Samuel French, depending upon country of performance. Please be aware that *FIN & EUBA, CLEAN, THE GULF,* and/or *STUCK* may not be licensed by Samuel French in your territory. Professional and amateur producers should contact the nearest Samuel French office or licensing partner to verify availability.

MUSIC USE NOTE

Licensees are solely responsible for obtaining formal written permission from copyright owners to use copyrighted music in the performance of this play and are strongly cautioned to do so. If no such permission is obtained by the licensee, then the licensee must use only original music that the licensee owns and controls. Licensees are solely responsible and liable for all music clearances and shall indemnify the copyright owners of the play(s) and their licensing agent, Samuel French, against any costs, expenses, losses and liabilities arising from the use of music by licensees. Please contact the appropriate music licensing authority in your territory for the rights to any incidental music.

IMPORTANT BILLING AND CREDIT REQUIREMENTS

If you have obtained performance rights to this title, please refer to your licensing agreement for important billing and credit requirements.

LOVE IS A BLUE TICK HOUND first premiered in 2016 at Birmingham's Terrific New Theatre (Tam DeBolt, Artistic Director) in the author's home state of Alabama in 2016. It was produced by Sandra Taylor, Jim Gordy, and Carolyn Messina. The Production Stage Manager was Cari Oliver and the Technical Director was Kathleen Crawford Jensen. The cast and directors were as follows:

FIN & EUBA

Directed by John McGinnis

FIN . . . . .Peggy Vanek-Titus

EUBA . . . . Donna Thornton

CLEAN

Directed by Bethe Ensey

LINA. . . . . Carolyn Messina

ROBERTO . . . . .John McGinnis

STUCK

Directed by Alan Litsey

BOB . . . . Barry Austin

MAGGIE. . . . . Jennifer Salvant

THE GULF

Directed by Tam DeBolt

KENDRA. . . . . Carolyn Messina

BETTY. . . . . .Rebecca Yeager

AUTHOR'S NOTES

ON STORIES OF HEALING

There exists a state of inertia—a kind of reckless apathy—that is worse than death itself. A place where souls go to die, even as we stand back and allow it: a thankless job, a bad marriage, a dysfunctional family. And although we are not truly "stuck," we often convince ourselves that we are, through some idea of wholeness, an idea of our own creation, an idea that may very well be full of holes. Getting out requires math (the hard kind): Why do we settle...and what is the full cost of leaving? These are the central questions in *Love Is A Blue Tick Hound*. Through four intimate duets—*Fin & Euba, Clean, The Gulf,* and *Stuck*—we witness all the many facets of love as the pairings form, flounder and fall apart. These pieces are my founding documents, so to speak. They are connected thematically and represent a sort of literal rendering of how I came to know myself as an artist.

ON AGE RANGES

I have devoted my writing life to creating challenging roles for both women and men. Although the characters in these one-acts may be played by people of any age or ethnicity, there is a certain heartache known only to those who have been scarred and kicked around by life. I strongly urge casting directors to consider actors of all ages, shapes and sizes for the roles in my plays.

ON SILENCE

When a text is stripped to its essence, it returns the gift of tension. Much of the story that would otherwise be inaudible reveals itself in these quiet moments. I strive to create dialogue that is free from extraneous noise and filled with the richness of silence and shadow. Listen carefully as you read these plays and you will notice that the characters—and the elements of the worlds that surround them—assert themselves in the hushed and quiet moments: the call of a distant factory whistle or the sound of cars driving by on the lonely highway in *Fin & Euba*; the deafening calm that follows the big fight scene in *The Gulf*; the tender story of the Little Tree in *Stuck*; and the delicate moments in *Clean* just after the journal is discovered. These stories are not to be rushed. Directors of my material should make note of the quiet moments and the beats, not as throwaway stage directions, but as an indicator that the silence is yet another character in the narrative—and that is has something to say.

ON INCLUSION

As a playwright—and as a member of the human race—I believe I am the best reflection of myself when I am championing the under-represented. I value, and so encourage, diversity and inclusion, both as a product and as a practice. By product, I mean my body of work. Thematically, the product often deals outright with elements of diversity. Additionally, in practice, casting, staging, and production decisions can and should reflect diversity whenever possible. I encourage flexibility in casting, especially with age-range and ethnicity. Herein, whenever explicit staging or production elements would preclude production or impede creativity, reasonable "work-arounds" and innovative approaches are encouraged.

FIN & EUBA

FIN & EUBA was first produced in Silver Spring, Maryland, where it won the 2003 Silver Spring Stage One-Act Festival. It subsequently won the Maryland One-Act Festival and the Eastern States One-Act Festival that same season. The production was directed by Michael Kharfen and the cast was as follows:

EUBA .... Erika Imhoof

FIN .... Audrey Cefaly

FIN & EUBA later debuted in New York where it won the 2006 Strawberry One-Act Festival. The play was directed by Joseph Holmgren and the cast was as follows:

EUBA .... Carolyn Messina

FIN .... Audrey Cefaly

CHARACTERS

EUBA: A woman of any age and ethnicity; quiet; a follower.
FIN: A woman of any age and ethnicity; self-assured; dry and gritty.

SETTING

The yard of an old boarding house in the deep South.

TIME

Autumn, late evening.

AUTHOR'S NOTE

Fin and Euba are poor and scrappy. They say and do things that may seem surreal or comical, but in all things there is a truth to their ways. They are not *caricatures*. That is to say, they are very real people with real problems. Every effort should be made to identify their core beliefs and to portray them honestly.

STAGING

The below elements are not a requirement for staging. Reasonable workarounds and text edits are encouraged to meet the needs of the individual production. Please submit any edit requests to Samuel French for prior approval.

Alcohol, Smoking, Open Flame

(SETTING: The yard of an old boarding house with an abundance of tacky yard art, gnomes and all things ridiculous. The house overlooks both a lonely highway and, in the distance, a paper mill. A porch light is visible near an area that represents the house.)

*(AT RISE: **EUBA** exits the house onto the porch. She goes through her nightly ritual of retrieving an old coffee can from under the porch and situating herself in a lawn chair so she can light a cigarette. She sorts through a small stack of mail. A letter draws her attention. She hides it hastily as **FIN** enters the yard.)*

FIN. Hey.

EUBA. Hey.

FIN. Can I bum one?

*(**EUBA** passes her the pack.)*

Where is she?

EUBA. Same as always. Back in the back watching Home Shoppin'.

FIN. God. Ain't she got enough of them creepy critters?

EUBA. They keep disappearing. She keeps buyin' more.

*(**FIN** points to a gnome and looks to **EUBA** for an explanation.)*

It's new. *Buddy.*

FIN. Buddy? They have *names?* Gross.

(They stare out at the highway. An occasional car speeds by.)

It's gettin' cold.

EUBA. Yeah.

FIN. Don't you think it's gettin' cold?

EUBA. Yeah, it's gettin' cold.

 (silence)

FIN. Bernice told me you got a letter in mail-call today.

 (beat)

 From *Life Magazine?*

EUBA. Bernice talks too much.

FIN. Well, ain't you gonna tell me what it says? You been waitin' for that letter since June.

EUBA. No.

FIN. No?

EUBA. I ain't read it.

FIN. Why not?

EUBA. Personal reasons.

FIN. What?

EUBA. Private reasons.

FIN. Oooh. Oh, I see. Okay. Alright. That's fine…you don't want to tell me.

EUBA. Good.

FIN. Your best friend.

EUBA. Yup.

FIN. The only person you could trust in the whole wide world.

EUBA. Yup.

FIN. But you don't want to tell me –

EUBA. Nope.

 (silence)

FIN. Shoulda worn my jacket.

EUBA. Mnnn hmn.

FIN. Two weeks till Thanksgiving, you believe that?

EUBA. Double shifts again next week.

FIN. You're kiddin'?!

EUBA. Fat Charlie told Thelma 'n' Thelma told me.

FIN. Good! I need the money.

EUBA. I need sleep more than I need the money.

FIN. That's the truth.

> *(beat)*

I heard something, but you ain't gon' like it.

EUBA. What?

FIN. Miss Vera's fixin' to raise the rent next month.

EUBA. Where'd you hear that?!

FIN. Bernice. Said she overheard her talkin' about it on the phone to Brother Herbert.

EUBA. Shit.

FIN. Yup.

EUBA. How much?

FIN. *(through an exhale of cigarette smoke)* I don't know.

> *(pause)*

EUBA. You know I'd move in a heartbeat.

FIN. Me too!

EUBA. Too many rules.

FIN. I know it!

EUBA. Better not let her see you smokin' out here. She'll kick us out for sure.

> **(FIN** *blows a defiant puff of smoke toward the house.)*

FIN. Let's do it.

EUBA. What?

FIN. Move.

EUBA. You're crazy.

FIN. I'm serious!

EUBA. It's too far, Fin. The next rooming house is two miles down. That's way too far to walk to work.

FIN. Lou Anne lives down there at Scooter's. We could ride in with her. And he ain't have no rules, neither, except cash only.

EUBA. Cash only?

FIN. Cash only. And no pets.

EUBA. No pets?

FIN. No pets.

EUBA. What about a fish?

> *(beat)*

Could I have a fish?

FIN. I bet you could have a fish.

EUBA. Maybe I'd like a fish.

FIN. What, like a goldfish?

EUBA. No, one of them pretty ones, with the pretty colors.

FIN. Oh yeah! I like them. Fish are good.

> *(beat)*

What do you think?

EUBA. I don't know.

FIN. I'll call Scooter tomorrow.

EUBA. *I don't know.*

FIN. We could think on it.

EUBA. Yeah…

FIN. Let's just think on it.

EUBA. Okay.

FIN. We'll just think on it. That's what we'll do.

EUBA. *(trying to close the subject)* Okay. Let's think on it.

FIN. *(overlapping)* Okay.

> *(beat)*

I'm thinkin'.

> *(silence)*

EUBA. We got any beer?

FIN. Hangin' off the dock out back!

> *(FIN exits.)*

EUBA. *(calling)* You better hope she don't find it.

FIN. I hope she does!

> (**EUBA** *pulls out the unopened letter and holds it, contemplating.*)

EUBA. *(to herself)* Stupid.

> (**EUBA** *looks at Buddy, who is staring back at her.*)

(to Buddy) Shut up.

> (**EUBA** *hides the note as* **FIN** *returns with the beer.*)

FIN. Shiiiiittt, these are cold!

EUBA. Well what do you expect, pond's about froze over.

> (**FIN** *hands* **EUBA** *a beer.*)

Damn!!

FIN. I told you.

FIN. Man…there's nothin' better!!

EUBA. Nope.

FIN. I love a good cold beer.

EUBA. *Really cold…*

FIN. You OK?

EUBA. Yup.

FIN. Ice headache?

EUBA. Yup.

FIN. Well drink some more, you'll be alright.

> (*A factory whistle is heard in the distance.*)

BOTH. 10 o'clock.

FIN. They got a new foreman comin' in next week.

EUBA. Where's Lila?

FIN. Fat Charlie sent her home. She couldn't keep up.

EUBA. When's the baby due?

FIN. Any day.

EUBA. How's she look?

FIN. She looks good. She looks real good. *Big.*

EUBA. I miss havin' her on my shift.

FIN. I know it. She's so funny. You remember back last fall when we had that real bad storm and everybody was down at Piggly Wiggly fightin' over toilet paper? Well, I saw Lila, Terrell and I don't know who all else, a big ol' crowd of folks standin' around Bobby Johnson's butcher counter cuz one of the stock boys had gotten all pissed off at Bobby one night and had went and built a Kotex Maxi-Pad display inside the meat case.

EUBA. I forgot all about that.

FIN. So Lila says, "That's a mighty fine display, Bobby. You havin' a special?" I'm gon' miss her.

EUBA. She'll be back.

FIN. Nuh uh! She's movin'.

EUBA. What?

FIN. Well, you remember how her husband went through basic training last summer?

EUBA. Yeah.

FIN. They just assigned him to a unit at Ft. Bragg and they're movin' soon as the baby's born.

EUBA. What?

FIN. She's mad as a hornet too. She just got the baby's room all fixed up and everything.

(The front porch light flashes.)

BOTH. *(ad lib)* Oh…Oh man…Shit.

(They hide their beers.)

FIN. *(to* **EUBA***)* Fifteen minutes. *(calling)* Yes, ma'am!

EUBA.	**FIN.**
(overlapping) God, I can't stand that woman!	*(overlapping)* She gives me the creeps! Her and them thirteen cats.

EUBA. *Seventeen.* Ginger had her litter this mornin'.

FIN. *(warning)* That's it! We're movin' to Scooter's'. I mean it, Euba! I'm callin' Scooter tomorrow. My hands are frozen.

EUBA. I'll get a blanket.

(EUBA exits into the house to get a blanket. FIN sips her beer quietly, looking around the yard. She goes over to Buddy, the gnome, and quietly picks him up. She takes him off stage and throws him into the pond. We hear a splash. She re-enters cavalierly rolling up her shirt sleeves.)

FIN. Oops.

(FIN notices that EUBA has left her letter behind. She casually picks it up and tries to decode it from the outside. She is nearly caught as EUBA returns.)

EUBA. *(calling back)* Yes ma'am! *(mimicking)* "Ain't you girls comin' in? I flashed that light a hundred times." Here, I stole you a cookie.

(EUBA hands FIN the blanket. She looks at the letter and then at FIN, who is casually looking away.)

FIN. Yumm. What'd you tell her?

EUBA. Nothing. I just looked at her. She was still yacking away when I left.

FIN. Yack. Yack. That woman could talk the chicken offa bone.

(beat)

I wonder how somebody could do that much talkin' and still not say anything.

(beat)

Euba?

EUBA. Yeah?

FIN. When you gon' open that letter?

EUBA. *Life Magazine* does not care about any of the stupid pictures I took in high school, Fin. Get real.

FIN. I didn't send 'em those, Miss Smartypants. I sent 'em the ones you took at the plant during the strike last summer.

EUBA. Whatever.

FIN. What if it's a job offer?

EUBA. *(overlapping)* Oh, get serious, Fin. You think you can just send my pictures to some big shot at *Life Magazine* and expect a job offer?

FIN. *(overlapping)* Oh, give me a little more credit, will ya? I did not just send them to any old big shot. I sent them to the *Executive Editor,* if you must know. I took his name right off the inside cover.

EUBA. Now, that makes all the difference don't it?

FIN. *(staring at* EUBA *blankly)* You are so negative. Negative. Negative. Negative.

EUBA. *(overlapping) Realistic.*

FIN. Yes. That too! And negative.

> *(beat)*

I bet it's a job offer! What do ya think?

EUBA. I don't know and I don't care.

FIN. Don't lie.

EUBA. I ain't lyin'. I don't want to know.

FIN. Why?

EUBA. It's better not knowing.

FIN. Better?

EUBA. I didn't send the pictures, Fin! You did!

FIN. It's what you wanted.

EUBA. No, Fin. It's what you wanted.

FIN. You said. You dreamed about it.

EUBA. No I didn't.

FIN. Don't lie! Euba. You have been dreamin' about taking pictures for *Life Magazine* ever since high school.

EUBA. OK, yeah, alright. Yeah I dreamed about it, but that don't mean I want it.

> *(beat)*

FIN. That don't make no sense, Euba. Dreamin'... wantin'...same thing.

EUBA. No, it ain't. Dreamin' is dreamin,' that's all it is. Wantin' means you're willin' to work for it and I ain't and that's all.

FIN. What are you talking about?

EUBA. Do I dream about it? Yes! Of course, I do. When I'm out there on that line all day and my feet are so swole up I can't think straight? I dream about it. Or when Bugger James comes into my room 'stead of his own at 4 a.m. cuz he's so blind from drunk. I dream about it. Or how 'bout, every mornin' scrambling for a warm shower 'stead of ice cold, cuz I slept in two minutes late. Fin, I dream about getting out every minute of every day of my life.

FIN. Well, what are you waitin' for? *(holding up the letter)* This is your chance, Euba.

EUBA. *(taking the letter)* Because. If I open this letter. And it says what I know it's gonna say…

FIN. What?

EUBA. …then I have nothin'.

FIN. But what if they want you!?

EUBA. What if they don't?

FIN. What if they do?

EUBA. What if they don't?! What if I open that letter, and it tells me I'm no better than anybody else in this –

FIN. Oh, come on!!! If I had half your talent, I'd march right down to that office and I'd tell that fat bastard Charlie to kiss my ass. I'd quit. With no notice! And I'd start walking till I hit Atlanta. And you wanna know what else?!?! *I wouldn't look back!!! I'd never look back!* Not even for you, baby. Not even for you.

EUBA. Well, thanks a lot.

FIN. It's nothing personal.

EUBA. I know it.

FIN. Open the damn letter!

EUBA. Stop it!

FIN. Euba!

EUBA. Leave it alone, Fin.

FIN. It's a sin what you're doin'. Throwin' away your God-given talent.

EUBA. How come you can't just drop it?!

FIN. You oughta be ashamed.

EUBA. Stop!!

FIN. No, I won't. And you wanna know why?

EUBA. Cuz you ain't got any dreams of your own, that's why!

> *(silence)*

FIN. *(stung)* Nice. Turn it back on me, why don't you?

EUBA. *(overlapping)* I didn't mean it, I'm sorry.

FIN. *(overlapping)* Oh, save it, Euba! I know what I want. And you can call it dreamin', wantin' *whatever*. Kids? Yep. On the list. One girl. One boy. And a husband someday, if I can find one who'll have me. Somebody to love. Somebody who will love me back. A white house, with a little wrap-around porch…on a little quiet street –

EUBA. *(overlapping)* Don't forget the white picket fence.

FIN. *(continuing defiantly)*—in a little quiet city—that don't smell like something dead. And just maybe, when I'm old and ugly, I want a blue tick hound dog named Jake…

> *(beat)*

…who knows his name, who will come when I call him, and who will love me, no matter what, cuz that's what dogs do.

EUBA. Sounds like you got it all planned out…

FIN. *(sincerely)* Yeah, well, I ain't special like you, Euba.

EUBA. Oh, come on –

FIN. *(overlapping)* No, no, it don't bother me. You bother me. You say you want a fish, but you don't even know what kind!

EUBA. Fish? Fish? We're talking about fish now? I know what kind of fish Fin, I just can't think of the name, that's all.

FIN. My point exactly.

EUBA. I know what I want.

FIN. No, you don't.

EUBA. Yes, I –

FIN. *(overlapping)* No! No you don't, Euba. You sit here and bitch and you moan about this place…about gettin' out. But it's all just words, idn't it? You never do anything. You never do anything about it.

EUBA. I'm happy right where I am, thank you very much.

FIN. Don't say that! Don't you ever say that!

EUBA. Leave it alone, Fin.

FIN. You know what –

> *(beat)*

Okay. Fine. Have it your way.

EUBA. I think I will. Thank you.

FIN. As long as you can live with it.

> *(beat)*

Come Sunday morning and you're sittin' there. Seventh row center at Southside Baptist. Trying to explain to the Good Lord why you took the gifts—the *gifts*—that he gave you and *threw them all away*! You hear me?!?! Just threw 'em away. Now what do you think he would have to say about that?

EUBA. I can't speak for Jesus, Fin.

FIN. Well, I can! And I'll tell you what he'd say. Shame. On. You! Shaammme on you, Yolanda Eubanks!

> **(EUBA** *quickly pulls out the letter and starts ripping it up.)*

Stop it! What are you doing?!?! Are you insane?!?! Euba!!

> **(EUBA** *holds a lighter up to the letter in warning. A cold, menacing demeanor washes over her.)*

EUBA. Get back, Fin. I'm warning ya. I got a Dale Earnhart Intimidator and I ain't afraid to use it.

FIN. You wouldn't!

(**EUBA** *flicks the lighter on.*)

EUBA. You wanna take that chance?

FIN. Don't do it. You'll never live it down, Euba.

EUBA. *(overlapping)* You better get back, Fin! Now, I need you to leave me be on this, you hear me?!?!

FIN. Euba, please!

EUBA. *Back away!*

FIN. Euba –

EUBA. I'LL TORCH IT!

FIN. I believe you would. I do. I'm backing away, see me, I'm back. Now put the lighter down.

EUBA. *(pointedly)* Now, this is *my* life. *MY* LIFE! And it's mine for me to decide if I want to throw it away, you got it?

FIN. Yes!

EUBA. No more *talk*! No more fish! No more nothin'!!

FIN. *(overlapping)* Okay. Yes. Yes. Okay. I'm sorry. Please… just…just…just…put the lighter down.

(**EUBA** *accidentally burns herself on the lighter. She drops the lighter and the papers on the ground.*)

EUBA. *(overlapping)* Ow! Shit!!

(*silence*)

(*a realization*)

I'm crazy…

FIN. No.

EUBA. I am. I'm crazy. That's the only explanation.

FIN. No. No.

EUBA. I mean it, Fin. Whatever this is, it ain't normal. It ain't—something's wrong with me.

FIN. Euba?

EUBA. *(overlapping)* I'm scared, Fin. You hear me? I'm scared!

FIN. Of what? A letter?

EUBA. No! Of…of everything. Afraid to go. Afraid to stay. Livin'. Dyin'. We're screwed, you know that? We're screwed! Stuck in this house with that crazy witch. No car. No phone.

> *(triumphantly)*

> *Beta fish!*

FIN. Beta fish! Yes!

EUBA. With no nothin', Fin, when you think about it. We work in a mill that spits poison twenty-four-seven. And the smell, God that smell. It turns my stomach, Fin. I can't get away from it. It's in my clothes, it's in my hair, it's in my sheets, Fin! It's in my sheets!

FIN. I know.

EUBA. I've probably got some sort of deadly disease eatin' away at me on the inside. For Christ's sake, Fin, we have to wait for a northern wind to barbecue! God, I hate it here! I hate this fucking place.

FIN. Then leave!

EUBA. What if the next place is no better? Ya ever thinka that?

FIN. Wha –

EUBA. What if the next place…is *worse* than this?

FIN. *(taking in her surroundings)* That's a scary thought, Euba.

EUBA. You make it sound so easy. Just pick up, go somewhere, do something. I know there's better places, don't think I don't know that, but Fin…I can't. I can't…move. I can't—I'm—I'm stuck.

FIN. You are NOT stuck. You listen to me. You are NOT stuck. Ain't none of us stuck!

EUBA. Yeah.

> *(beat)*

> I am.

(The porch light flashes another warning. **EUBA** *hurls a beer can towards the porch.)*

EUBA. OH, SHUT UP!

(She falters, gasping for breath.)

Oh, God, I can't breathe!

FIN. Shh shh...okay, okay, caaallmmm down. Calm down.

EUBA. I AM CALM!!

FIN. Okay, well calm down a little bit more for me, then.

EUBA. Okay.

FIN. Take a deep breath.

EUBA. Okay.

FIN. Take another one, sit down here for a second and catch your breath, where's that beer? Whooaa, whooaa. Okay, now keep breathing, don't forget to breathe. Everything's gon' be back to normal here, now just keep breathing.

EUBA. Okay.

FIN. Here, have a drink.

*(***EUBA*** *drinks.)*

Alright?

*(***EUBA*** *nods.)*

Have another sip. Alright. You okay?

*(***EUBA*** *nods. Silence.)*

It's tough. I know. But...it might help if you remember...God never gives us more than we can handle.

*(***EUBA*** *slowly turns and stares blankly at* **FIN.***)*

FIN. *(backpedalling)* Well sometimes. Sometimes he does. Sometimes, it is just a little bit more than we can handle. But that's why we have each other.

*(***EUBA*** *takes a deep swig of her beer. She gathers the pieces of the letter and stands for a moment looking*

down at them. She is resolved now. She lights the papers. As they burn, she takes a cigarette out of the pack and lights it from the flame. She throws the burning pieces into the coffee can. **EUBA** *sits and stares out at the lonely highway.*)

(silence)

EUBA. *(vacantly)* Fin?

FIN. *(stoic)* Yep?

EUBA. What happened to Buddy?

FIN. He went for a swim.

EUBA. Oh?

FIN. Yeah.

(silence)

(**FIN** *puts the blanket around her and grabs her beer and sits. The lull of the crickets and heaviness of the air envelope them both. They resume staring out at the lonely highway.*)

(defeated) It's gettin' cold out here.

EUBA. *(an apology)* Yeah.

FIN. Don't you think it's gettin' cold?

EUBA. Yeah.

(beat)

Yeah…

(silence)

…it's gettin' cold.

(Lights fade to blackout.)

End of Play

CLEAN

CLEAN was first produced in Silver Spring, Maryland, where it won the 2009 Silver Spring Stage One-Act Festival. It subsequently won the Maryland One-Act Festival and the Eastern States One-Act Festival that same season. The production was directed by Leta Hall and the cast was as follows:

ROBERTO . . . . Nello DeBlasio
LINA . . . . Erika Imhoof

CLEAN later debuted in 2011 in New York, where it was a finalist for Emerging Artists Theatre's summer EATFest. The play was directed by Troy Miller and the cast was as follows:

ROBERTO . . . . Matt Stapleton
LINA . . . . Glory Gallo

CHARACTERS

LINA: A waitress. Any age. A disheveled woman who looks older than her years.

ROBERTO: An immigrant. A dishwasher. Any age. A gentle soul, prone to bouts of exuberance. The part may be played 'as is' (Italian—with broken English) or in any other language that is well-suited to the actor's range. (As such, language substitution within the text is permissible.)

SETTING

A restaurant. Anywhere.

TIME

Present day.

(SETTING: 2 a.m. An empty restaurant, after closing time.)

(On one table there are napkins and cutlery being prepped for the next day. There is a mop bucket on the floor and chairs are turned up for cleaning.)

(AT RISE: LINA lies on the tiled floor. Her apron is dirty and her work shoes are old and worn. She is weeping softly and cradling a mop.)

(ROBERTO appears in the doorway with his backpack and keys. He is shocked to see LINA on the floor.)

ROBERTO. Lina! What is this?

LINA. Tell me the truth.

ROBERTO. *Che?*

LINA. *(lifeless)* Does this mop make me look fat?

ROBERTO. Lina, please tell me what's happen?

LINA. *What's happen...*

ROBERTO. You fell?

LINA. I'm doing my pilates.

ROBERTO. Pilates?

LINA. This maneuver is quite complicated, actually. It works your inner core and your...ass fat, area.

ROBERTO. *Scusa* [excuse me]?

LINA. Yes, Roberto, I fell.

ROBERTO. I call the nine one one.

LINA. No!

ROBERTO. Are you hurt?

LINA. No.

ROBERTO. Can you get up?

LINA. No.

ROBERTO. What can I do?

LINA. I just want to lay here.

ROBERTO. Lay here?

LINA. Yes…

ROBERTO. Okay…

>   (**ROBERTO** *stands to leave.*)

LINA. STAY!

ROBERTO. Okay…

>   (**ROBERTO** *moves closer.*)

LINA. I woke up this morning, Roberto…I got out of bed. I looked in the mirror…and I realized…I am so fucking old.

ROBERTO. No, *bella.* You are not –

LINA. *(overlapping)* Yes I am. And please don't argue with me, it works better that way.

ROBERTO. *(overlapping)* Lina…no…

LINA. *(overlapping)* I am lying here like roadkill on this disgusting floor and I am having the worst day of my life. Okay, maybe not the worst day, but it's gotta be up there. Top five for sure. Did you see that crazy woman fighting with her husband, the one with the hyena voice, the one that kept laughing at her own jokes?

ROBERTO. Oh, *sí!*

LINA. *Sí,* yeah. Her. She threw a plate of pasta at his face, Roberto. His face!! From across the table! Fettuccine went flying. What is wrong with people? And what is wrong with water? Just a glass of water in the face, right there in the face, two, three ounces, tops. It's simple, it's classic…good for the environment.

>   *(beat)*

It wasn't supposed to be like this. Ya know what you never hear Roberto? Here's what you never hear…in kindergarten, when Mrs. Tipton looks around at those cute little innocent faces and she says…*kids, what do you want to be when you grow up? Oh, oh, I know! I wanna be a waitress! I wanna grow up and clean up after other people's problems ALL day long, and oh, please, I want that hyena lady, cuz I just love scraping pasta off the ceiling!*

> *(beat)*

You never hear that Roberto. You never do.

ROBERTO. I'm sorry you have this bad day, Lina.

> **(ROBERTO** *lays down by her side.)*

> *(silence)*

> *(noticing the underside of the table)*

ROBERTO. Oof!

LINA. Disgusting.

ROBERTO. My God!

LINA. Fifty years of Hubba Bubba…

> *(beat)*

ROBERTO. *Hubba?* Ah ooba booba?

LINA. *(amused)* Ooba booba, yes.

ROBERTO. *(enthralled)* Ah, *sí!* Remarkable!

LINA. The yellow one has flavor crystals. It sparkles…

ROBERTO. *Flavor crystals…*

LINA. Just once, I want my life to be like it is in the movies, ya know…like—like a fifty dollar tip or somebody wins the lottery. You ever notice how the waitress in the movie always ends up with the good guy in the end? I could be in the movies. Just tell me what to sign, I'll sign it. I'll sign anything.

> *(beat)*

You don't have to stay. I'm fine now.

ROBERTO. *(skeptical)* Hmm…

LINA. I am.

> *(They do not move.)*

> *(silence)*

This is the most we've spoken. Ever. Why is that?

ROBERTO. *Boh* [I don't know].

LINA. How long have you worked here?

ROBERTO. We start on the very same day. Eh…five years and three weeks.

LINA. Five years? Please don't tell me we've been doing this for five years, Roberto.

ROBERTO. And three weeks.

LINA. Can that be true? Oh my god. Aren't you tired?

ROBERTO. *Sí.*

LINA. Then why do you stay? Don't answer that.

ROBERTO. Why?

LINA. Because then you'll ask me why I stay, and I won't be able to answer you, except to say that I have no idea.

(*beat*)

Seriously, why do you stay?

ROBERTO. (*shaking his head*) *Non lo so* [I don't know].

(*beat*)

You did a good job with the mopping. Looks good.

LINA. (*heartfelt*) *Thank you* for noticing. No one ever does.

ROBERTO. I do.

LINA. You do?

ROBERTO. *Sí.*

(*beat*)

LINA. I like to mop…

ROBERTO. Why?

LINA. Because…because it's *mine*. No matter what kind of day I've had, it's the one thing that's mine. And I do a damn good job too. I put the chairs up—no one else does that. Late at night…everyone is gone. It's the last thing I do after silverware and wipe-downs and sugar and ketchup. I start at the counter, and I wind my way around A3 and A4 and then I backtrack behind the waitress station, and back through B and then C, and then I mop myself into a little corner and out the door. I turn the key, and when I look back in the window, I can see everything—my whole day—shiny and...*clean.* And it makes me feel like anything, no matter how far gone...can be new again. Is that weird?

ROBERTO. No.

LINA. No?

ROBERTO. Do you not think it is, eh...human nature to want order...to...want to make sense of a life? Maybe this mopping is not the best way, but eh, if it works for you...

LINA. My father told me I could be anything. And I believed him...for a really long time. And you, a *dishwasher.* Let me guess...a lifelong dream, right?

ROBERTO. No.

LINA. Tell me.

ROBERTO. What?

LINA. The story. *Your* story.

ROBERTO. Ah. It is boring.

LINA. No.

ROBERTO. It is a *ninna-nanna* [lullabye/bedtime story]. You will fall to sleep.

LINA. Please.

ROBERTO. Ah, well...my father was a *contadino*...eh... farming? But, eh, we did not see eyes to eye.

LINA. No?

ROBERTO. No. Difficult man. He could not, eh, read... write...mah, the one thing that he knows is terra... eh...the land. And eh, the farm...this was all he ever knows. I love him, but I cannot live this life. To stay in one place, never to see the world, no. *Non per me* [not for me]. And one night, I tell him this, I say these things to him. He have this look in his eye. This is the very bad part.

(*beat*)

Mmn...

   (beat)

He will not forgive me, so...I cannot stay.

LINA. So you left...

   (beat)

Don't you miss him?

ROBERTO. *Sí.*

LINA. You're very brave...

ROBERTO. Eh...not too much.

LINA. Do you ever think of going back?

ROBERTO. No. This is where I must be.

LINA. You mean...America?

ROBERTO. Eh...no.

LINA. No?

ROBERTO. Sometimes in your life, you have...eh, how do you say, a porpoise? Porpoise?

LINA. *(instructing) Purpose?*

ROBERTO. Ah, *sí, purpose*—what is this? Purpose?

LINA. Umn...it's like...when you have a *reason* for something.

ROBERTO. *Sí, sí.* This is purpose. *Sí.* Do you know how something will keep you? *Ti mantiene* [keeps you]?

LINA. Keeps you?

ROBERTO. *Sí.*

   (pointing to his heart)

It keeps you...

LINA. Oh. Yeah. I do.

   (beat)

So you're happy...

ROBERTO. Eh...

LINA. What?

ROBERTO. *Happy...*

   (silence)

LINA. You know, Roberto, I saw you last week.

ROBERTO. Oh?

LINA. At the farmer's market.

ROBERTO. The market?

LINA. You didn't see me?

ROBERTO. No...

LINA. What—you looked right at me.

> *(beat)*

I had on an orange dress...

ROBERTO. No.

LINA. Strange. You were buying tomatoes. Heirloom tomatoes.

ROBERTO. Ah, *pomodori* [tomatoes]? You did not say hello.

LINA. I didn't want to disturb you. I just wanted...to observe you...in your natural...habitat.

ROBERTO. *(amused)* Habitat? Like in the zoo? If you want to see me in a zoo, you would not have to go this far!

LINA. No, I just mean...well, it was nice to see you out in the open. Away from here, ya know?

ROBERTO. *Sí.*

> *(beat)*

Maybe...eh...

LINA. What?

ROBERTO. Maybe you see me, is okay you say hello.

LINA. Oh?

ROBERTO. I cut you a tomato, we go for a walk.

LINA. A walk?

ROBERTO. *Sí...*eh...along the river.

LINA. That sounds nice. Do you have many girlfriends, Roberto?

ROBERTO. No!!!

LINA. Oh, I bet you do.

ROBERTO. I do not.

LINA. It's okay, don't be embarrassed.

ROBERTO. I do not. I have no time!

LINA. No time! What an excuse!

ROBERTO. Well…I do have my eye on someone.

LINA. You do?

ROBERTO. *Sí*, but eh…she is far away.

LINA. Oh. I'm sorry. I'm sure she is very special.

ROBERTO. *Sí*. And what about you?

LINA. No.

ROBERTO. No?

LINA. No. I'm done. I am through with all of that shit. Love…men, all of it.

ROBERTO. No! Why do you say this?

LINA. What, that I'm through with love, the fairy tale? When you stop believing in *happily-ever-afters*, Roberto, you can't be disappointed when there isn't one.

ROBERTO. Pff.

LINA. What?

ROBERTO. This is no way to look at your life, Garrincha!

LINA. *Garrincha*. Why do you call me that?

ROBERTO. It is a problem?

LINA. It is a problem, yes, Roberto. You've got the whole kitchen calling me that.

ROBERTO. Garrincha! Most famous *calciatore* in all of Brazil, aside from Pelé of course.

LINA. Of course!

ROBERTO. I call you Garrincha, out of respect. He was a survivor, and so are you.

LINA. He died of cirrhosis of the liver! In his fifties.

ROBERTO. How do you know this?

LINA. I Googled.

ROBERTO. *Googood?*

LINA. GOOGLED! I don't like it.

ROBERTO. *Bella.* This is upsetting to you?

LINA. Yes. Yes, it is upsetting to me.

ROBERTO. If you want me to stop, I stop.

LINA. Thank you.

>   *(beat)*

ROBERTO. I cannot!

LINA. Yes you can.

ROBERTO. No!

LINA. Roberto.

ROBERTO. No.

LINA. Why not?

ROBERTO. It is how I see you.

LINA. As a drunk, middle-aged, dead soccer player?

ROBERTO. Yes. NO!! No, no, *Bella...*

LINA. Then what?

ROBERTO. Two years ago, you come to work, you're upset, you have a new pair of eh, brown eh—*pantaloni*—eh... *trouser.* You say *Roberto...look at my feet.* I look at your feet. You say to me *do you see anything unusual?* I say... *No...I see two feet.* You say to me, *Roberto! Clearly! My left leg is shorter than my right.* And I say to you, Lina, *this is ridiculous, your legs, they are the same.* And you give me this look in your eye...

>   *(off* **LINA***'s look)*

THAT ONE! Right there, that's the one...and you take the tray *così (slamming an invisible tray),* and you walk away, and we never speak of this again. But I keep in my mind...and then one day, I remember. *Garrincha. Sí,* the drinking and the women, yes, but more than this, he had the one leg, *six centimeter* shorter from the other, and still he becomes LEGEND!

>   *(beat)*

LINA. Are you serious?

ROBERTO. Legend!

LINA. Okay...as much as I adore that comparison—and I do, I really love that—umn...I am not a legend, Roberto. I am a waitress with a dirty apron and aching feet –

ROBERTO. *(overlapping) Dai! Non dire cazzate* [don't talk crap]!

LINA. *(suddenly aware of how dirty her hair is)* ...and pasta in my hair, Roberto!!! Do you see this?

ROBERTO. Ah! You are like the oobah boobah! You have a flavor crystal!

LINA. Why can't you let me be miserable?

ROBERTO. Okay!

> (**ROBERTO** *holds out his hand to* **LINA.**)

LINA. No...

ROBERTO. Up!

> *(He helps her up and into a chair.)*

Okay! And now, you sit. Sit, sit. SIT!

> (**LINA** *sits.*)

I don't want to hear no more of this crazy things. Okay?

LINA. Did I mention I'm crazy?

ROBERTO. *BASTA!!* NO MORE OF THIS! And don't you laugh at me! I give you something to laugh about, for sure! This is no joking! You push me to the limit!

LINA. Sorry to bother you with my problems.

ROBERTO. No, no, no, no...I don't care if you bother, Lina, this is not the point. But you won't listen to the reason. You want to go on believing these crazy idea of ugly, eh...hopeless, *boh*. What else for me to say, eh? I could say to you look, Lina, it is a beautiful blue sky, and no, you contradict!

LINA. Because sometimes, Roberto...IT ISN'T! SOMETIMES, IT RAINS PASTA!!!

ROBERTO. Ah...my life, a devastation. *Porcoddio* [swearing], I want to kill myself with a salad fork!

(**LINA** *rakes her arm across the table, sending silverware flying.*)

LINA. GO AHEAD!

(*silence*)

(**ROBERTO** *picks up a fork and walks toward* **LINA**. *He leans over her, threatening with the fork.*)

ROBERTO. Your life has *meaning*, Lina.

(**ROBERTO** *slams the fork down on the table and takes the mop from her hands. He begins to mop with a vengeance.*)

(*silence*)

LINA. I'm sorry...

(*beat*)

I don't know why I did that, I don't usually throw utensils, it's really not my thing.

(*beat*)

Why do you care, anyway? It's not like you've taken any interest before. You just sit there *(gesturing to his preferred table)* every day with that notebook. That stupid notebook.

ROBERTO. *(mopping)* No! This is not stupid!

LINA. Well, whatever it is, it's all you seem to care about. You barely speak to me. All this time we've been here, we have the same lunch break every day and you barely speak to me.

ROBERTO. We're speaking now!

LINA. It doesn't count!

ROBERTO. *(mopping more intensely now) Che cazzo ma queste donne sono tutte uguali* [women are all the same]. You're all the same. *Women!* They want you to listen, but not too close. They want you to hear them but no respond. *Quindi se sei stupido* [when you are stupid]...if you are stupid like me...and don't respond, they accuse you of *not listening!*

LINA. You missed a spot.

ROBERTO. *(furiously mopping the "missed'"spot)* Per l'amor di dio [For the love of God]! GOD FORBID if you do respond, if you try to offer a suggestion: MORTO!

> (**ROBERTO** *throws the mop across the room in disgust.*)
>
> *(silence)*

It's not that I do not want to speak to you, Lina. I try to speak...

LINA. *(a realization)* You did see me at market, didn't you?

ROBERTO. Some things, eh...difficult to say.

> (**ROBERTO** *takes a moment to gather his courage and then reaches into his back pocket to pull out his notebook. He opens the book and then reads aloud.*)

On Fri...

> *(beat)*

On Friday, you walk from the library, I notice your shoe is not tied...but, eh, you do not tie it...

> *(to* **LINA***)*

You leave it this way for two hours, I remember this clearly...

> *(returning to the journal)*

And then, you see here on Tuesday...you...

> *(gesturing to her preferred table)*

You have a book. And you sit with the morning light. There is, eh...

> *(reading)*

Juice, pancake—three pancake—oatmeal, grits, bacon, sausage, eh...and eh...two eggs, over easy, on toast.

LINA. Holy shit.

ROBERTO. *(in agreement)* This is a big breakfast.

LINA. *(reaching for the journal)* Please?

>   (**ROBERTO** *holds tightly, but then relents.*)

LINA. *(reading aloud)* You read Tennessee Williams, something about a Cat on a Roof, I think maybe you like cats...I like cats too...

>   *(to* **ROBERTO***)*

You've been stalking me?

>   *(long pause)*

ROBERTO. *Sí.*

>   (**LINA** *turns a few pages.*)

LINA. *(reading aloud)* Did she see me? I do not know. I hide behind the tomatoes...

>   *(beat)*

She walks down Canal Street. She eats a tangerine, the color of her dress. It is the color of the sun and she lea— she leaves me without air. Without the air to breathe. I walk a step behind and hide in lonely doorways...

>   (**LINA** *flips back to the first page of the book.*)

>   *(reading aloud)*

Twenty-nine October, Lina works late. She looks ti –

>   *(beat)*

She looks tired. She looks...

>   *(to* **ROBERTO***)*

Twenty-nine October. My birthday...

>   (**ROBERTO** *nods.*)

There was a cupcake...in my locker...

>   (**ROBERTO** *nods.* **LINA** *is overcome.*)

ROBERTO. *(comforting)* Ssshhh...shhh...shhh...

>   *(silence)*

Bella. You are not old. And you are not…

LINA. What?

ROBERTO. You have…fettuccine in your hair…but to me… you are the most beautiful…I watch you every day from the window. *Bella.* But, I cannot speak to you. It is a long time I did not have the language. And, eh, the years come, I begin to learn English, but still, I cannot find these words. So, I…I put them *nel libro* [in the book], on the paper. Maybe they mean something…

> *(beat)*

Maybe they mean nothing, *boh.* I say too much. *Mi dispiace* [I'm sorry].

> (**LINA** *reaches for his hand.*)

Lina.

> *(beat)*

I might…eh…fall into pieces.

> *(beat)*

Speak to you? Lina…there is nothing in the whole world I would rather do than speak to you…

> (**LINA** *kisses his hand.*)

Except maybe to kiss you…kissing would be better, no?

> *(beat)*

You are in my mind, all of the day and I cannot get rid of you. It is you, Lina. You are the reason I stay. *Capito?*

> *(They kiss.)*

LINA. *Sí.*

> *(They kiss once more.)*

> *(Lights fade.)*

End of Play

THE GULF

THE GULF was first produced in Silver Spring, Maryland, where it won the 2010 Silver Spring Stage One-Act Festival. The production was directed by Chris Curtis and the cast was as follows:

BETTY . . . . Erika Imhoof

KENDRA. . . . . Audrey Cefaly

THE GULF later debuted in New York, where it won the 2015 Samuel French Off Off Broadway Short Play Festival. The play was directed by Joseph Holmgren and stage managed by Emma Ruopp. The set was designed by Sylvia Nicole Allan and the cast was as follows:

BETTY . . . . Effie Johnson

KENDRA. . . . . Carolyn Messina

CHARACTERS

BETTY: An optimist. A thinker. Restless and tender-hearted.
KENDRA: A loner. Scrappy, dark, brutish and volatile.

SETTING

A fishing boat. Alabama delta.

TIME

Autumn, late evening.

(On a quiet summer evening, somewhere down in the Alabama Delta, **KENDRA** *and* **BETTY** *troll the flats looking for redfish.)*

*(***KENDRA*** *slowly reels in the line while* **BETTY** *lies with her feet in* **KENDRA***'s lap, reading* What Color is Your Parachute: A Practical Manual for Job-Hunters and Career Changers. **KENDRA** *sighs…)*

BETTY. What?

KENDRA. Nothin' but rats.

BETTY. Huh?

KENDRA. Man…some *scrawny* rat reds tonight…

BETTY. Kinda bait you using?

KENDRA. Baby, if the fish ain't bitin it ain't cuz of the bait.

    (beat)

It's cuz they ain't there.

BETTY. Wan' go somewhere else?

KENDRA. Nope.

BETTY. Rosella was talking about over by Bottle Creek.

KENDRA. Bottle Creek?

BETTY. I told her we were comin' out here.

    (beat)

She was bein' helpful.

KENDRA. Rosella has no idea about fishin' and therefore Rosella is not helpful.

BETTY. What's wrong with Bottle Creek? Can't fish in Bottle Creek?

KENDRA. Yeah, for boots and dead bodies.

BETTY. I thought there was good fishin' there.

KENDRA. Well there was, but not no more.

BETTY. How come?

KENDRA. BP Fuckers.

BETTY. BP?

KENDRA. That shit got in…choked it.

BETTY. Aw shit…

> *(beat)*

You know…you got the whole Gulf of Mexico to fish in, we always end up here.

KENDRA. What are you sayin'?

BETTY. Right here in the shallows, every time.

KENDRA. That's the whole point.

BETTY. I don't get it.

KENDRA. Exactly.

BETTY. What?

KENDRA. That's where the—nevermind.

BETTY. No, tell me. Please.

KENDRA. Fish in the shallows, cuz that's where the fish are.

> *(beat)*

Reds like to fight, Betty, they fight…deep,shallow, whatever, any water. But in the shallows, they get more traction, see, the fight is bigger…more fun.

BETTY. For you, maybe.

> *(beat)*

KENDRA. When did you talk to Rosella?

BETTY. Last night…

> *(beat)*

It's warm, idn't it? I might hop in for a swim if I didn't think the gators would get me.

KENDRA. Assuming they'd want you.

> **(BETTY** *returns to reading her book.)*

BETTY. *(off* **KENDRA***'s look)* What?

KENDRA. Nothin'.

BETTY. Why can't I do what I want to do? You're doin' your thing.

KENDRA. Fishin' boat, not a library.

BETTY. I could fish if I wanted to, I ain't in the mood.

>   *(beat)*

I know how to fish. I do!

KENDRA. When did you ever fish?

BETTY. When I was little. Caught my first fish when I was eight years old. It counts! It does! Stop it, stop laughin'.

KENDRA. What'd you catch?

BETTY. Sunfish.

KENDRA. Sunfish?

BETTY. Little ole Sunfish. Daddy said to me, now Betty, the rule is…you catch it, you gotta clean it. And then I found out what cleaning was and I thought I don't want to have nothin' to do with that.

KENDRA. So what'd you do?

BETTY. I just put him in the well, there, under the boat… laid there watchin' him. I can't do it. I can't do what you do. You…gut those fish wide open like it's nothin'. That catfish last week, his little heart just floppin' all over the boat, why you reckon it does that?

>   *(beat)*

You caught that fish, took out the *insides,* the heart is just layin' there, it's still beatin', Kendra. The fuck… why'st do that?

KENDRA. *(playfully)* Cuz it loves me. Even in death it loves me. It's what I got, I can't help it.

>   *(beat)*

So what'd you do with him?

BETTY. Who?

KENDRA. Sunfish.

BETTY. Oh…umn…I just picked him up by his tail and put him back in the water. He didn't move none at first, he just laid there, like he was dead or somethin. I put my little finger on him and he made a ruckus and swam off. Back to his family.

KENDRA. *Back to his family.*

BETTY. His family—whatever—you're bein' mean!

KENDRA. I ain't bein' mean. You always think I'm bein' mean, I'm just listenin'.

>   *(beat)*

BETTY. *Whatever.*

KENDRA. Oh here we go...look at this asshole...

BETTY. Who is it?

KENDRA. Oh, my god. Will you look at that? What kinda dumbass comes out to fish the flats in a shit-tub like that...

>   **(KENDRA** *tries to make out whose boat it is.)*

>   *(calling)*

Duke?! What the fuck are you drivin' man, you just got paid or what? Oh, I'm sure the fish love it, they be floatin' up dead at the sight of it.

>   *(to* **BETTY***)*

Stupid fuck.

>   *(to Duke)*

Man...you know what? You can make fun of my coon-ass boat package all you want, but we'll see who's up by the end of the night, won't we? You should try up by Bottle Creek...

BETTY. *(overlapping)* Kendra!

KENDRA. *(continuing)* Oh, hell yeah. Redfish, gars, trout, whatever, fulla surprises, that Bottle Creek.

>   *(beat)*

Would I lie to you? Move along Duke, you're spookin' my fish...

>   *(to* **BETTY***)*

Say goodbye Betty.

(They lazily shoot the bird at Duke as his boat rides by. **KENDRA** *notices Thelma in the back of the boat.)*

KENDRA. *(to Thelma)* Hey Thelma!

*(***KENDRA** *turns to see that* **BETTY** *has pulled out a small picnic basket and is assembling some fancy fixings for a snack.)*

KENDRA. What the fuck is that?

BETTY. *(defensively)* This is all the same food that you eat every other day of the week, only today it is newly configured into this creative combination for our little fishing excursion.

KENDRA. You gon' answer my question?

BETTY. Tapanade.

KENDRA. *Tapanade.*

BETTY. Olive tapanade. Garlic, capers, basil, lemon. All chopped up.

KENDRA. OK, so…olives?

(They glare at each other, as if in a stand-off. **BETTY** *holds up another option…)*

BETTY. Canapé.

KENDRA. That is not a can-a-paint or whatever the fuck word you're sayin', that there is a Ritz cracker with some kind of bullshit green distraction, something like a Vienna *(pron: Vai-yee-ner)* sausage and a snot drop of Cheez Whiz on top.

BETTY. Snot drop? That's disgusting.

(beat)

Are you serious right now? You know what, you remind me of like some kinda Neanderthal cave man except without any of the social skills. Actually, I take that back. You are like a Neanderthal cave man with just enough social skills to kind of blend in to your *sewage plant* surroundings, but I would say even that is a bit of a stretch.

(beat)

BETTY. Hello?

> (**KENDRA** *busily digs into the cooler for another beer.*)

I don't even know why I bother…

> (**BETTY** *starts packing up the food.*)

…try to educate you…broaden your horizons, and you are basically a twelve-year-old boy.

> *(beat)*

What are you doing?

KENDRA. *(busily doing something else)* I am over here not giving a fuck about anything coming out of your mouth.

> *(beat)*

BETTY. Do you listen to yourself when you talk? Do you hear the things you say or—you know what, forget it.

> *(beat)*

For the record, Kendra…that there is andouille sausage, or maybe you've heard of it, *arugula* and fucking aged Wisconsin cheddar, which looks nothing like the barbaric mutation that is Cheez Whiz. Because A, it's not melted, and B, it's just sitting there, not melted. If it was Cheez Whiz—which it NEVER WILL BE—it would look a little different, now wouldn't it? It would look –

KENDRA. *(overlapping—deadpan)* Like a snot drop?

> *(beat)*

BETTY. You see me here holding this piece of cheese, Kendra? This is my kryptonite. I am immune to you and all of your mean-spirited mental terroristics.

> (**BETTY** *pops the piece of cheese into her mouth, staring at* **KENDRA** *defiantly as she chews it.*)

KENDRA. That's your kryptonite?

BETTY. Yep.

KENDRA. You're ingesting your own kryptonite?

BETTY. Yep.

KENDRA. Just checkin'.

BETTY. *(regarding the cheese)* God-DAMN that's good.

> *(**BETTY** pulls out her book and resumes reading.)*

> *(beat)*

KENDRA. Oh, good. That's good. Let's read a book. Let's all read a book.

BETTY. *(reading aloud) Theoretically, you could be just as happy as a garbage collector.*

> *(to **KENDRA**)*

They have the least amount of stress as any job, you know that? I read that someplace. And think about it. What do they have to be stressed about anyway, except maybe, you know, some maggots and dead rats and whatnot?

KENDRA. I don't know.

BETTY. And you know what…I bet after a couple weeks even the maggots would just be routine, whaddya reckon? Alright, now here is a list of possible occupations, however, this is in no way—here it says—*no way intended to be a definitive list, but more a list of suggestions based upon your core competencies and desires.*

> *(beat)*

I'll just read the list.

KENDRA. *(seriously annoyed)* Please.

BETTY. *(reading)* Prison guard.

> *(beat)*

KENDRA. *Prison guard?*

BETTY. Yep.

KENDRA. *(incredulous)* You added my whole life up on that worksheet there and that's what came out?

BETTY. I may have added a few ideas of my own.

KENDRA. Like prison guard…

BETTY. Yeah, like prison guard yes, like a lotta things, are you gonna keep an open mind or maybe we'll just quit all this, how bout that? This book *helped me,* K. It's how come I know what I wanna be now, and before I was just driftin around and whatnot.

KENDRA. Good for you.

>*(beat)*

BETTY. Are you jealous of me?

KENDRA. *(increasingly frustrated)* Could we be more different? I wonder.

BETTY. Well, what does that mean?

KENDRA. Look, this is *your dream,* not mine, this *social working* whatever, and I want you to go to school. I do. I'm proud of you...

BETTY. *(overlapping)* Why won't you come with me?

KENDRA. We have been through this.

BETTY. It's junior college, not forever.

KENDRA. Exactly.

BETTY. Well, I don't like the idea of us bein' apart, do you?

>*(beat)*

>*Hello?*

KENDRA. What?

BETTY. You gotta see the world sometime. What are you gonna do, fish the rest of your life?

KENDRA. Well, I don't know, is it on the list? Why do I need a parachute, anyway? What the fuck is that?

BETTY. It's not an *actual* parachute.

KENDRA. Just a *pretend* parachute.

BETTY. It's a *metaphor.* Do you remember me tellin' you that about twenty minutes ago?

KENDRA. Uh...I think I'd remember a pretend parachute.

BETTY. Well, I guess so, especially when you're stuck somewhere WITHOUT IT!

>*(digging in)*

>Welder. Mechanic. Dairy Queen Manager. That was a test...to see if you were listenin', are you listenin?

KENDRA. *(overlapping)* Yes, god, yes!

BETTY. Wedding planner.

KENDRA. Fuck off!

BETTY. Mortician.

> *(beat)*

What?

KENDRA. *Mortician?*

BETTY. You can thank me for that one.

KENDRA. Mortician?

BETTY. Only because I know how much you like dead people.

> (**KENDRA** *stares at* **BETTY** *as if she has three heads.*)

That's how come you watch that show all the time, with the "Y" incision.

KENDRA. Dr. G –

> *(beat)*

Dr. G…is not a mortician, Betty. Dr. G is a medical examiner for the city of Orlando—that's a good one, actually, medical examiner, write that down—and I don't watch that show for the dead people, okay, I told you that.

BETTY. *(playfully)* Have you got a crush on Dr. G?

KENDRA. Just write it down!

> (**BETTY** *freezes for a moment, retracing their steps.*)

BETTY. Oh, shoot. I got that kryptonite thing backwards, huh?

KENDRA. Yep.

BETTY. Shit.

> (**BETTY** *notices* **KENDRA***'s knife laying nearby. She picks it up and turns it over in her hands, caressing the blade.* **KENDRA** *is wildly aroused by this…*)

KENDRA. You gon' cut me open?

BETTY. I was thinkin' about it…

KENDRA. Let's do it.

BETTY. *(staring at the blade)* How long does a fish heart keep beatin'after you…ya know…

KENDRA. 3.2 seconds.

BETTY. 3.2 seconds?

KENDRA. I don't know Betty! I never counted, Jesus Chist with the fish hearts!!

BETTY. Don't be mean.

KENDRA. I'm not bein' mea—stop trippin'—give me the knife!

> *(beat)*

I want you to stop thinking.

BETTY. Why?

KENDRA. Because when you think, I'm miserable!

BETTY. Why won't you think about it? You been sayin' you need a change, you been sayin' you hate it here.

KENDRA. It's just talk.

BETTY. No it ain't.

KENDRA. It's only 100 miles away, Betty. What's the big deal anyway?

BETTY. Well it just seems to me you ain't happy and maybe this could be a shot at something different, something good.

KENDRA. Could we move on, please, to some topic I give a shit about? I ain't gon' choose my calling offa some list you got from a self-help book.

BETTY. This is a career-path *workbook*, Kendra. What color is *your* parachute?

KENDRA. Red.

BETTY. It is not red. It is not at all red, and if you had been listenin', you would know that. We are on chapter nine, Kendra. *Geography of the Heart.*

KENDRA. Is that the last chapter? I sure hope it is.

BETTY. *(overlapping)* You are being obtuse.

KENDRA. Absolutely, I'm being obtuse –

BETTY. *(overlapping)* Do you even know what that means –

KENDRA. I would *love* to know what that means!

BETTY. It means somebody who is smarter than hell, but who is set on pretending to be *dumber than shit* so maybe nothing is ever expected of 'em and then they don't have to do anything but sit around and fish for all eternity. How's that sound?

KENDRA. *(beat)* Is that a trick question?

BETTY. Do you have a plan? For your future?

KENDRA. Will you stop?

BETTY. Do you?

KENDRA. I had a plan. Yeah. I had a plan to do a little drum fishin', maybe catch a bull red or two and not have to deal with ridiculous questions and psychotic-analysis, how's that for a plan?!

BETTY. *(overlapping)* I will never understand you.

KENDRA. Thank GOD for that!

BETTY. Open…your mind!

KENDRA. To what?

BETTY. The future.

KENDRA. I have a job.

BETTY. That's not a job…

> *(beat)*

You work at a sewage plant.

KENDRA. Oh, and your job is saving lives, I guess. Is that it?

BETTY. Well, yeah, actually, it is, if you wanna know. I do save a life from time to time. Jenny Jessup gave me some of her nitro pills to keep under the bar, just yesterday afternoon, in case she ever goes into cardiac arrest. I keep a box of condoms under there, Trojans… for Bobby Lee, right next to the margarita mix and the rock salt. Swear to god, it's a damn pharmacy under there. You wouldn't believe the shit I see. These folks, they come in there…half of 'em want to get laid, half of 'em want to get drunk and the other half just need to talk. And it ain't in my job description, but I do it, cuz that's what bartenders do…they listen. I listen to 'em and you know what I hear?

(beat)

Desperation. Quiet desperation. So quiet, only dogs can hear. In the eyes, the shaky voice. Starin' down at the ice cubes in the glass, like readin' tea leaves or some shit. I pour 'em one on the house, I look 'em square in the eye, and I ask 'em the same thing I'm askin' you.

(beat)

Oh, come on K, can't you open your mind and think about it. I mean is it really that hard to imagine? No, seriously. If you could be anything at all in the whole wide world, what would it be?

KENDRA. Alone.

BETTY. Oh, shut up. You couldn't be alone no more than I could. You can't even sleep with the light off.

KENDRA. I'm afraid of the dark now, is that it?

BETTY. Afraid of somethin'…

KENDRA. *(overlapping)* Oh my god!

BETTY. You sleep with the light on…you fish in the shallows…

KENDRA. And you speak Chinese, the fuck are you talking about? I'm…I'm afraid to live or some shit?

BETTY. Maybe. Maybe you are.

KENDRA. And you don't know how to sit still, how about that? Nothing's ever good enough for you, is it? We came out here to *fish.* But you never fish, Betty.

BETTY. Yes, I do.

KENDRA. *(overlapping)* You don't. And you don't want to learn, either, you just want to sit there with your books and your papers and whatnot, and rearrange *my life* to make it fit yours in some magical futuristic happy place that exists—where? I don't know, in your mind, maybe? Meanwhile, I'm doin' it. I'm taking part in the miraculousness of life, Betty. REAL LIFE. Where folks catch fish, rip their FUCKING guts out and then eat 'em. And they don't think twice about it and you wanna know why? Cuz it's just FISHIN'!

BETTY. Do you love me?

KENDRA. *(a warning)* I'm 'on lose it.

BETTY. Do you?

> *(inching closer and closer to* **KENDRA***)*

Sex ed teacher…underwear model…massage therapist.

KENDRA. Yes. I love you.

BETTY. I love you too.

> *(They kiss.* **KENDRA** *pulls open the folds of* **BETTY***'s blouse to kiss her neck…)*

KENDRA. You smell like roses…

BETTY. Mmn…

KENDRA. Wait.

BETTY. God I love you.

KENDRA. What is that?

BETTY. What?

KENDRA. What is that smell?

> *(beat)*

I fuckin' knew it.

BETTY. K…

KENDRA. You been up to Butler county, hadn't you? You been up there with her? And now you're sittin here with me, parachute bullshit trying to straighten out my fucking life. That is some fantastic shit.

BETTY. I was putting an end to it.

KENDRA. In person? God. FUCK! I'm such an asshole.

BETTY. It's not what you think.

KENDRA. *(mimicking) I've changed, K, I've changed.*

BETTY. I have.

KENDRA. Oh, please. You are still the same slut I met at Mardi Gras.

BETTY. Yeah, well you took to it pretty quick as I recall.

KENDRA. What are you gonna do, Betty?

BETTY. About what?

KENDRA. *About your fucking life!* You can't keep that shit locked up for two seconds? Howlin' all over town like some bitch in heat. And you stink too, Betty, by the way. You need some feminine hygiene. All our time together, six years I gave you, took you back, took the BITCH back, WHY? Why the fuck did I—junior college?! I'm gon' pack up my shit and go with you to junior college?! That is fuckin hilarious. I'm done. I am beyond done.

> (**KENDRA** *grabs* **BETTY**'s *backpack.* **BETTY** *reaches to take it from her.*)

LEAVE IT! Leave it.

> *(menacing)*

Get outta the boat.

BETTY. K…

KENDRA. Get. Out. Of the boat.

> *(beat)*

What?! What the hell do you want from me? Can't you tell I hate you? Can't you tell I hate your fat ass?!

BETTY. No you don't.

KENDRA. Oh, I do! I do! You are killin' me. I want you to go. I want you to just get your shit and go…PLEASE. I can't do this no more. You wanna know the truth? I'm glad you're leavin'. I been wantin' you to leave since July! You are bad for me…you are bad for my soul, Betty.

> (**KENDRA** *starts throwing* **BETTY**'s *things overboard.*)

BETTY.	**KENDRA.**
K, please, stop, stop…	Out…get out…out, out, out…

BETTY. K! I love you!

> (**KENDRA** *looks at* **BETTY** *a moment and then violently pushes her overboard.*)

KENDRA. OUT!

> (**KENDRA** *grabs whatever she can find and begins throwing it all at* **BETTY** *who is floundering in the shallows behind the boat.*)

KENDRA. OUT, out, out!!!! And take this psycho-shit with you.

Maybe there's a chapter in there about skanks and the morons that love 'em.

> (**KENDRA** *throws the book overboard.*)

Where's that parachute now, BITCH?! That ought to break ya, huh? Egg-suckin' dog.

> (**KENDRA** *collapses exhausted into a heap inside the boat.*)

Damn Betty. You wear me out!

> *(long silence)*

> *(The soaking wet book flies back into the boat.* **KENDRA** *remains motionless. A hand reaches up and grabs the side of the boat, then another, then a foot, as* **BETTY** *crawls back in.)*

> *(silence)*

BETTY. Kendra…

KENDRA. *(a lifeless syllable)* Hmn…

BETTY. I think maybe you have some pent-up hostility toward me.

KENDRA. How'd you guess that?

BETTY. I'm sorry, K.

KENDRA. *(a whisper)* Why do you do it?

BETTY. What?

KENDRA. Why do you do it?

BETTY. I wish I knew. I ain't never been any other way. I could never understand it myself 'til that time my cousin told me I had codependence. And then I started to think on it and that's when I realized maybe she was right 'cuz it did seem like I had somethin' wrong with me to where I always needed somebody, you know, like the thought of being by myself was…do you hate me?

KENDRA. *(numb)* Yeah.

> *(Childlike,* **BETTY** *rather shakily situates herself in the boat and leans back to look up at the night sky.)*

BETTY. One fish, two fish, red fish, blue fish. This one has a little star, this one has a little car, say what a lot of fish there are.

> *(beat)*

You ever sit and think about your life in reverse…like back to that second when it was all just exactly the way you dreamt it could be?

KENDRA. No.

BETTY. You walked into the Judge Roy Bean's on Fat Tuesday. 'Member that? I was sittin' there at the bar and I looked up and saw you…holy shit. Leather jacket…snake-skin boots. Thirty pounds of Mardi Gras beads hanging off that rack of yours. How's you get all them beads anyway?

KENDRA. Offa some Baylor boys…

BETTY. Baylor?

KENDRA. I just went up to a group of Baylor boys and I asked real nice.

BETTY. What you say?

KENDRA. Hand 'em over.

BETTY. And they just gave 'em up, huh. Just like that.

KENDRA. Yep.

BETTY. Out of the kindness of their hearts.

KENDRA. *(overlapping)* Yep.

BETTY. You had your tits out didn't ya?

KENDRA. All the way out.

BETTY. You flashed 'em good, didn't ya? I'm surprised they didn't go blind.

KENDRA. Few of 'em did.

BETTY. That was it for me. That night. I know I'd never love nobody like you. And I hadn't. All these years.

KENDRA. I just wish I was enough.

BETTY. You are.

KENDRA. You are so ridiculous.

BETTY. What?

KENDRA. That's the difference between us. You ain't never gon' be happy with me.

BETTY. I –

KENDRA. No. Face it.

> *(beat)*

We gotta go…

BETTY. Go where?

> **(BETTY** *touches* **KENDRA**'s *hand…)*

You've always had the prettiest hands…

> *(beat)*

I feel like we're disappearin'…

KENDRA. Sssshhh. Let's just sit here for a while. Tide starts movin'…we'll catch a few.

> *(beat)*

I'm sorry about what I said…

BETTY. About what?

KENDRA. Feminine hygiene.

BETTY. Oh.

KENDRA. You smell good to me.

> *(beat)*

BETTY. 3.2 seconds…

KENDRA. I just made that up.

BETTY. I know you did. But…how long, though. If you had to guess…how long before it stops.

KENDRA. Maybe a minute…

> *(beat)*

BETTY. A whole minute? Wow. Does it just stop or does it slow down and then stop.

KENDRA. Slows down a bit.

BETTY. Why does it do that…

KENDRA. What's that?

BETTY. Why does it keep beating like that…

> *(beat)*

KENDRA. Habit.

> *(silence)*

> (**KENDRA** *drinks down the last drop of her beer and tosses her can into the corner of the boat. She casts her line once more into the shallows.*)

BETTY. *Pet psychic. Meter maid. Dental hygienist.*

STUCK

STUCK was first produced in Silver Spring, Maryland, where it won the 2011 Silver Spring Stage One-Act Festival. It subsequently won the Maryland One-Act Festival and the Eastern States One-Act Festival that same season. The production was directed by Audrey Cefaly and the cast was as follows:

MAGGIE..Andrea Spitz

BOB ....Jose Guzman

CHARACTERS

BOB: neurotic, self-conscious, a people-pleaser.
MAGGIE: decisive and charismatic.

SETTING

Maggie's apartment, an eclectic explosion of color, one that says "life."

TIME

Early evening.

(AT RISE: Lights up. Curtain music continues over a prelude.)

(MAGGIE enters her living room. She is barefoot and wears a lovely summer dress. She anxiously straightens the pillows on the sofa and goes to peer out a window for something. She exits back into the bedroom.)

(BOB enters the street outside MAGGIE's apartment...he has a note in his hand. He is looking for an apartment. He is lost. He looks around, confused. He exits off.)

(MAGGIE re-enters, now wearing heels and adjusting an earring. She leaves a newspaper on the table and checks once more out of the window. She scurries off.)

(BOB re-enters the street, this time more convinced of the address. He checks his note...compares it with the house number, stuffs the note in his pocket, straightens his jacket and summons the courage to knock on the door.)

(Music fades, as...)

MAGGIE. It's open!

(BOB attempts the door. It is stuck. He knocks tentatively again.)

It's open!!!

(BOB struggles once more with the door, but this time it's personal: man against door. MAGGIE enters the living room and goes to the door. She struggles with the door from the inside as BOB struggles from the outside.)

MAGGIE. It's open...or is it...is it stuck?

(The door opens. **BOB** *stumbles in.)*

Ah, yes, you have to...there's a trick to it.

BOB. I was invested...I was...so close!

(They hug nervously.)

MAGGIE. How are you?

BOB. I'm good!

MAGGIE. *(a greeting)* Bob!

BOB. *That...*you look...

MAGGIE. Too much for a second date?

BOB. Is this our second date, I guess it is, huh? Feels like a first.

MAGGIE. Oh, I know, right? Coffee was nice, but this is... sort of...real...

BOB. Exactly. You look amazing.

MAGGIE. It's a thrift store dress.

BOB. It's beautiful...you're...beautiful...

(She blushes.)

(Regarding the house.)

BOB. Wow...

MAGGIE. Isn't it great? The windows...all the light.

BOB. It is...it's great.

MAGGIE. I fell in love with it instantly. I moved in last summer, had it painted...unpacked...three days later.

BOB. So quick.

MAGGIE. Yeah, ya know, I'm a very decisive person...so. I promised myself after the divorce I would be...we can say that word, right, divorce...yeah. Well, life's too short to be...wishy washy.

BOB. Right!

MAGGIE. I think that's why I was so attracted to you, Bob. You seem like such a decisive person.

BOB. I am. I am!!

MAGGIE. To tell you the truth Bob, a decisive man…

BOB. …decisive…

MAGGIE. …a man who isn't afraid to take risks…

BOB. …risks…

MAGGIE. …really turns me on.

BOB. *(decisively—deadpan)* I could not agree more.

MAGGIE. Is it hot in here?

BOB. Stifling.

MAGGIE. Something cold?

BOB. Yep.

MAGGIE. To drink?

BOB. Yep.

MAGGIE. OK.

BOB. I would definitely like something cold to drink. Definitely.

MAGGIE. *(highly aroused)* Don't. Go. Anywhere.

> (**MAGGIE** *exits to the kitchen and* **BOB** *exhales for the first time since entering the apartment. He is on fire, pensive and nervous, eager to play along with the decisive man routine. He removes his jacket to cool off.)*

> *(from offstage)*

MAGGIE. I thought maybe we could get some coffee and then head out to the movie.

BOB. Sounds perfect.

MAGGIE. *(from offstage)* The movie section is on the table there. Do you see it?

BOB. Yeah.

MAGGIE. *(from offstage)* Which movie did you want to see?

BOB. *(panicked—buying time as he skims through the movie listing)* What's that?

MAGGIE. *(from offstage)* Which movie?

> (**BOB** *locates the newspaper and scrambles to pick one at random.)*

BOB. *(calling)* "Memoirs of a Geisha."

    (to himself) Shaa...shit.

        (Long pause. **MAGGIE** *enters.)*

MAGGIE. ..."Memoirs of a Geisha"?

BOB. At the Uptown?

MAGGIE. *(suspicious)* ..."Memoirs of a Geisha"?

BOB. Definitely.

MAGGIE. Really?

BOB. Yep.

MAGGIE. Are you sure?

BOB. Positive.

MAGGIE. That's kind of a...chick flick.

BOB. *(a million meanings)* Is it?

MAGGIE. *(handing him his drink)* Are you patronizing me?

BOB. Patronizing...No. No!

MAGGIE. *(somewhat defensively—self-conscious)* Huh. I mean, I don't claim to be a professor of literature or quote poetry all the time like some people I know, but I know a few things.

BOB. I really want to see it.

MAGGIE. *(suspiciously)* OK...

    (MAGGIE *takes a small sip of her water,* **BOB** *drinks most of his in the first gulp.* **MAGGIE** *is amused. She smiles at him. He smiles nervously back.)*

"Memoirs of a Geisha"...

BOB. "Memoirs of a Geisha."

MAGGIE. You surprise me more and more Bob. I feel like there is this connection between us...do you feel it?

BOB. I do. Even before our first date...in that stupid chat box, ya know, I felt it. I did.

MAGGIE. Me too.

BOB. *(calculating)* I feel…no…I *believe*…when you see something you want…something you *really* want…you should –

MAGGIE. Take it…

> *(***MAGGIE*** *breathes in sharply. She moves a few inches toward* **BOB**. *He moves a few inches closer to her.)*

BOB. Otherwise…if you hesitate…

MAGGIE. Yeah…

BOB. …if you…hesitate…

MAGGIE. *(breathless)* …yeah…

BOB. Poof.

> *(***MAGGIE*** *snaps out of her trance and laughs nervously, but her heart is racing a mile a minute.)*

MAGGIE. Bob…

BOB. Maggie…

MAGGIE. I have an idea.

BOB. *(turned on)* Ideas…are so…good.

MAGGIE. This may seem a bit forward…

BOB. Nah…

MAGGIE. I mean I know we've only just met and all…

BOB. Yeah.

MAGGIE. But I would really like to do something to you…I don't think it's too soon…but if you think it is…or if you're not into it, you know, you can just say…Maggie, I'm not into it, and I would totally understand.

BOB. *(disbelieving—laughing softly)* Not into it…OK.

MAGGIE. We could even have a safe word.

BOB. *(slightly nervous—but smiling all the same)* A safe word?

MAGGIE. In case things get out of hand.

BOB. Out of hand. Heh.

MAGGIE. Close your eyes.

BOB. *(He closes his eyes.)* Close my eyes.

MAGGIE. Don't move.

BOB. *(dying)* Nope!

> (**MAGGIE** *removes her earring from her ear and places it in* **BOB**'s *hand. He feels it, recognizes it.*)

MAGGIE. Will you let me pierce your ear Bob?

BOB. *(opens his eyes widely)* My –

MAGGIE. *(covering his mouth with her hand)* Before you answer...I want you to know...I think piercings are like...the most profound statement of self that a person can make to the world. Well, aside from tattoos, which I adore...but that will come later.

BOB. *(muffled)* Later?

MAGGIE. And I just think...I just think...we have such a close connection already Bob...

> *(moving closer)*

and you can totally say no, if you want, but I really do think...

> *(even closer)*

I think it could be the beginning of something totally amazing between you and me, and I...

> *(They come inches from kissing...)*

BOB. Let's do it!

MAGGIE. Really?

BOB. Absolutely.

MAGGIE. Oh, Bob, do you mean it?

BOB. Quickly.

MAGGIE. *(elated)* Ohh!!! OH, wow! Oh, oh my gosh, OK. Oh...you will not regret this. I promise. OK, let me just go get my needles!

> *(clapping)*

YAY!

> (**MAGGIE** *exits for supplies.*)

BOB. *(calling weakly—more to himself)* Needles?

MAGGIE. *(from offstage)* I thought about getting one of those kits.

> **(BOB** *gulps down all of his water and then drinks down all of* **MAGGIE**'s.*)*

BOB. *(through the gulping)* Mnn hmn…

MAGGIE. *(from offstage)* But then I figured, I have everything I need right here, why bother with the expense.

BOB. Why bother. You didn't mention the piercings…in your profile.

MAGGIE. *(from offstage)* I didn't?

BOB. No. No, I don't think you did.

MAGGIE. *(ftom offstage)* I probably should have. I bet it would totally scare some men.

BOB. I bet it would.

MAGGIE. *(from offstage)* But not you Bob!

BOB. *(to himself)* Not me…

> **(MAGGIE** *breezes through the living room to the kitchen.)*

MAGGIE. I just have to get a towel for the blood.

> **(BOB** *collapses forward, head between knees, hyperventilating.)*

MAGGIE. *(from offstage)* You OK in there?

BOB. *(calling)* Great!

MAGGIE. *(from offstage)* You can turn on some music if you want.

BOB. *(calling)* I'm good!

> *(to himself—wiping his sweaty palms)*

I'm good. I'm good. I'm not good…not good, this is not good. Not good.

MAGGIE. *(entering with supplies)* I'm back!

BOB. Oh good!

MAGGIE. *(beaming)* You are so cute!

BOB. *(petrified though smiling broadly)* And you are sooo… prepared.

MAGGIE. Oh, yes! Of course, prepared! *Hello.* OK, you hold this. Just put this over your lap. Oh, by the way, are you a bleeder?

BOB. A bleeder?

MAGGIE. Well, you know some people bleed a lot. I tend to clot pretty easily, but everyone's different.

BOB. Uh, I would say, yeah, I'm probably a…

MAGGIE. A bleeder?

BOB. Yeah.

MAGGIE. Hey, it doesn't bother me any! Kind of adds to the experience if you know what I mean!

> *(**MAGGIE** arranges all of her supplies…and brings them out of her tool box in order of pain-infliction capability. A bottle of alcohol, a razor…)*

BOB. *(looking at all the tools)* …adds to the…experience.

MAGGIE. And now for my secret weapon.

> *(She pulls a red bliss potato out of her pocket.)*

BOB. Produce!

MAGGIE. Red Bliss!

BOB. *(smiling)* That is…that's a potato.

> *(**MAGGIE** quickly gets to the task of cleaning his ear and the needle with the alcohol.)*

MAGGIE. I got my first piercing when I was thirteen. I had wanted a piercing for so long…ever since Jenny Bartell had one in the third grade and I thought, I want to be just like Jenny and I begged my mom, I begged and begged. And she said Mags, if you make straight A's all semester, on the day you turn thirteen, I'll take you to get it done. So…all winter long I thought about it… and all through the spring. And Jenny and I snuck over to JC Penny and hid behind the makeup counter so she could point out the earring lady with the ruby lips. Even in that lab coat, you could tell she had really great tits but Jenny said they were bought with Daddy's money. And I remember wondering what kind of dad would buy his daughter fake tits. Well...anyway...I got my grades up...even in civics which almost killed me, but I did the extra credit work and got an A minus, which is still an A, no matter who you argue with and I would have fought it too, only Mom said...*straight A's, Maggie, I'm just so proud.*

(**MAGGIE** *has an emotional moment remembering her mother.* **MAGGIE** *puts the potato behind his ear and takes his hand and puts it on the potato to hold it in place.*)

What a day it was!

(**MAGGIE** *jams the needle into his ear like a skilled surgeon.*)

There we go. Woop...hold the towel.

(**MAGGIE** *quickly removes the potato and pushes the towel up to his ear. She continues with the story and does not see the look of agony on* **BOB**'s *face.*)

And I wasn't scared at all. It did hurt a little, but I didn't care. Then the lady with the ruby lips asked me, little girl, which earring do you want and I looked down at all the shiny little gemstones and I thought...how will I ever decide...

(*to* **BOB**)

You OK?

(**BOB** *gives* **MAGGIE** *a "thumbs up" though she still cannot see his face because the towel is in the way. He begins clutching at the afghan.*)

...but there was one little blue sapphire off to one side...with a tiny rose petal wrapped around it, and I thought it looked just like how I felt inside...and you know, a piercing should really be a reflection of you... right? Otherwise, why do it?

BOB. Why do it?

> (**MAGGIE** *pulls the towel away from* **BOB**'s *ear.*)

MAGGIE. Oh, wow! You are a bleeder! I'm surprised it didn't hurt more! Aren't you surprised?

BOB. Oh, I'm surprised!

MAGGIE. *(applying alcohol)* You OK?

BOB. I'm great.

MAGGIE. There we go...now it won't get infected.

BOB. *(in agony but hiding it)* What a relief.

> (*She puts the earring in his ear and sits back and admires her work.*)

MAGGIE. Oh, wow. Wow.

> (*She holds the mirror up so he can see it. He smiles broadly to make her happy. She looks at him. He smiles at her.*)

Thank you. Thank you for trusting me.

BOB. No problem.

> (**MAGGIE** *begins to exit...while wiping her needle.*)

MAGGIE. Does it hurt?

BOB. No, no, nope...not at all...

MAGGIE. *(from offstage)* Well that's good!

> (**BOB** *goes into an apoplectic John Ritter fit of pain...flopping over furniture as if being chased by bees.*)

I am just amazed at how well that went. Aren't you?

BOB. Yep.

MAGGIE. You wanna go for coffee?

> (**BOB** *trips over something, wounding himself even further.*)

BOB. Coffee...

MAGGIE. *(from offstage)* What's that?

BOB. *(more an expletive than a noun)* Coffee!

(**BOB** *collapses onto the sofa into a fetal position, slowly cocooning himself into the afghan.*)

MAGGIE. *(from offstage)* Great!

(entering)

Bob! Are you—what is it?

BOB. Pain. So much pain.

MAGGIE. It's hurting?

BOB. I think I broke your sofa.

MAGGIE. What did you...what...

BOB. This blanket is very soft...

MAGGIE. Bob...

BOB. I just wanted you to like me.

MAGGIE. What?

BOB. *(weakly—as if losing consciousness)* Where am I?

MAGGIE. Bob! BOB!

BOB. Maggie...

MAGGIE. What's happening? It's not bleeding, are you...

BOB. Not bleeding...

MAGGIE. No, it's not bleeding...

BOB. Afraid...

MAGGIE. Afraid?

BOB. Afraid of...

MAGGIE. Of...

BOB. Afraid of...everything.

MAGGIE. Everything?

BOB. Needles. Potatoes. Chick flicks, those, too.

MAGGIE. Chick flicks?

BOB. I was just trying to...I wanted you to like me.

MAGGIE. Bob...what are you...

BOB. The truth is...

MAGGIE. What...

BOB. You scare the SHIT outta me.

MAGGIE. I scare you...wait...what?

>   *(beat)*

I came on too strong. The needle, the piercings...oh, god. Why didn't you say something?

BOB. I come from weak people.

MAGGIE. Oh, my god, I'm mortified.

BOB. No, it's OK.

MAGGIE. This is not right, Bob, you should have stopped me!

BOB. I should have.

MAGGIE. *(She smacks him hard with the nearest pillow.)* What were you thinking?

BOB. I –

MAGGIE. Damnit Bob! So not cool!

BOB. I'm sorry...

MAGGIE. *(She begins pummeling him with the pillow.)* Really? Really, Bob? Am I that frightening? She's a freak—stay back, there's no telling –

BOB. *(overlapping)* Stop it! You're not frightening...you're just...big.

MAGGIE. BIG?

BOB. *(overlapping—hastily—covering)* Personality. Big personality.

>   *(beat)*

MAGGIE. Really feeling the love here, Bob...

BOB. No...you're not getting it...you're not...just...you're beautiful and smart and yes, charismatic...I love all those things about you...

MAGGIE. You do?

BOB. Yes. I do. I'm just trying to keep up...

>   *(silence)*

MAGGIE. *(suddenly very self-aware, sheepish)* I don't mean to be terrifying, that's not even me, shit, I was just responding to—I thought you were into it!

BOB. *(softly)* I was.

>*(beat)*

Well, not technically.

>*(beat)*

Not really at all, actually. But I liked your story. I didn't want to disappoint you.

MAGGIE. But Bob...that's...that's not what I...I don't want a man to...to...bleed for me, I want him to...I want...

>*(beat)*

Fuck. I knew I'd screw this up!

BOB. No...

MAGGIE. I'm no good at this...

BOB. Neither am I! You know how many coffee dates I've had this month? Twelve! I repel people!

MAGGIE. Oh, please.

BOB. They know me at Starbucks, they make a drink just for me. It's half vodka.

MAGGIE. That's not true!

BOB. OK, I bring the vodka.

MAGGIE. Good idea!

BOB. There's no rule, Maggie. There's no one way or the wrong way, you can do it all wrong and it'll still be OK.

MAGGIE. You don't talk like other guys

BOB. No?

MAGGIE. No.

BOB. What do they say?

MAGGIE. "Later."

BOB. Oh, I know that one.

MAGGIE. I'm sorry I screwed it all up.

BOB. OK, first of all, even if we never work out, or screw everything up, right—all the things—it would take both of us working together to do that, so stop it. And second of all, even after all that, I would still want to sit here with you.

MAGGIE. Why?

BOB. Because I like you, Maggie. You're real. And funny. And high on some cocktail that reads like…like joy and hope and that…condition people get when their heart is too big.

> *(beat)*

I want to be close to that. I want to be close to you.

MAGGIE. You do?

BOB. I'm here, Maggie. I'm still here. You stabbed me in the head and I'm still here.

> **(BOB** *holds out his hand to her. They sit.)*

> *(silence)*

MAGGIE. You have blood on your shirt.

> **(BOB** *inspects the stain.)*

BOB. Oh, actually, that's hot sauce.

MAGGIE. *(amused)* You're nice.

> *(beat)*

(looking down at her feet) Hmm. I forgot to paint my fourth and fifth toenail.

> *(silence)*

I feel like that little tree in the middle of the forest… all the other trees get cut down around it…and it's still sitting there…all by itself…crooked and lonely…and you look at it and you think, what a silly…little…tree. But it's still a tree. It's still a tree, it's just…out of place in the place where it's always been. Like…getting out of prison and discovering cell phones and…*decent people.*

> *(He pulls her close.)*

Sometimes I feel…

BOB. Shh…

MAGGIE. I feel…

> *(He holds her.)*

BOB. It's OK...

MAGGIE. I feel...

BOB. Maggie.

MAGGIE. I just want to feel normal again...

BOB. *(tenderly) Normal.* I don't even know what that is. What is that anyway? Normal. Is that like saying not good, not bad, somewhere in the middle with a healthy degree of self-loathing? And is that with or without the medication?

MAGGIE. *(emphatically)* With.

BOB. They should just call it what it is...it's not normal... it's not high, it's not low, it's just...mediocre, it's just middle. That's the ideal now, that's what we're aiming for...don't cry, don't sulk, or sink into any abysses of any kind, don't stand out, or raise any flags or alarms or think of anything brilliant or scream or violently shred anything into tiny pieces, just follow the crowd and blend. Once a day, in the morning, with food.

MAGGIE. *(lifeless)* My cat is on Zoloft. She had trouble adjusting to the new surroundings. I couldn't argue with her. Isn't this a great date?

BOB. What is the worst part of internet dating?

MAGGIE. The people?

BOB. *(in agreement)* Right? Right?? You know the drill! Some far away coffee house, not local of course, far enough away so they can't stalk you later. No last names, no first names, no phone numbers, too risky, just a note, a time and a place...and maybe, if you're lucky...eventually, she's sitting there across the table looking *remotely* like her *(air quotes)* "recent" profile pic, and she's talking... and she's talking...and you think...how old am I...or... wow, I thought I was bad off...or...she's way out of my league and she knows it. Any minute now she's gonna bolt. She'll have some appointment she forgot about or some conveniently timed text message from the friend she has on standby if it all goes bad. And me wishing I had a standby...waiting with a shotgun to put me out of my misery.

MAGGIE. *(lifeless)* We could make a suicide pact.

BOB. *(shaking his head)* I'm not reliable.

> *(They share a laugh.)*

MAGGIE. Do you think I'm out of your league?

> *(beat)*

BOB. No. I thought so at first...but now I think you're just like me. When I first saw your profile...I was just... blown away. So pretty, that picture, where has she been, can she spell, oh, look, *commas.* And then when I saw you in person, I thought...

MAGGIE. What?

BOB. I thought...you looked like some angel...I wanted to...well, I wanted to not fuck it up, basically.

MAGGIE. Bob. I don't want you to be scared of me.

BOB. I'm not –

MAGGIE. *(overlapping)* No listen...seriously...at the movie theater, I eat the average amount of popcorn and I turn off my cell phone and I've never been shooshed. Ever. And...on long walks I don't...I don't trip joggers or run into traffic...

BOB. So what if you did...what if you did? I can't even parallel park. You think I don't come into this with my own pile of shit? Everyone's fucked up, Maggie. Everyone. I'm damaged. You're damaged.

MAGGIE. I think I'm more damaged.

BOB. OK, whatever...we're both damaged, right? But, we're here now, and we're broken, so we deal with it. I feel...inadequate, too nerdy, you feel lost...you feel... like a...what is it...a little tree in the woods...identity crisis...this I can deal with. But let's agree...OK...let's agree right here and now...to just do us. BE us.

MAGGIE. You think the little tree has an identity crisis?

BOB. Identity crisis, whatever, no, actually, you know what? I think that little tree is perfect. Perfect and waiting. *Oh, little tree. Who found you in the green forest and were you* *very sorry to come away?* E.E. Cummings. I don't know all of it.

MAGGIE. Who?

BOB. It's a story…a poem, actually…I always preferred it to "Night Before Christmas," my brother and I would argue back and forth.

MAGGIE. Oh. So it's about a Christmas tree.

BOB. Well, sort of. But to me, it's more about…survival, maybe…no, *redemption.* There's this…perfect little tree…alone…waiting…and along comes this family… and they take the little tree home and they put her in a warm, safe corner with a really great view of the city. And they give her a blanket for her feet and a star –

MAGGIE. *(overlapping)* It's a she? The tree is a she?

BOB. *(overlapping)* Shhh, it's a she, yes, a she, and a star for her hair…and they gather up all the golden threads and shiny ornaments and give them to the little tree to hold…so then the little tree is happy…and beautiful… and loved. And no longer alone.

MAGGIE. No longer alone?

BOB. No.

> *(They kiss softy.)*
>
> *(They release, stare at each other a moment.)*
>
> *(They kiss again as lights fade.)*

End of Play